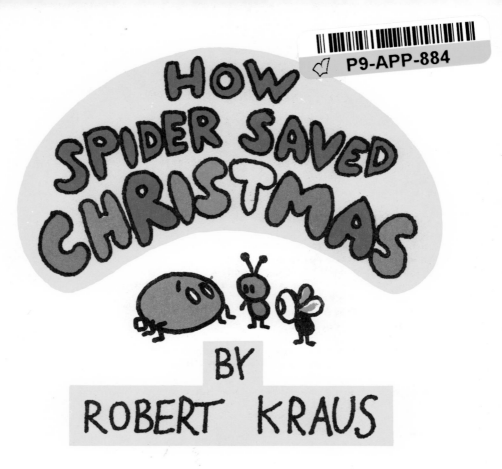

HOW SPIDER SAVED CHRISTMAS

BY ROBERT KRAUS

WINDMILL BOOKS and SIMON&SCHUSTER
NEW YORK

for Bruce, Billy and Pamela

Copyright © 1970 by Robert Kraus
All rights reserved
including the right of reproduction
in whole or in part in any form
Published by Windmill Books, Inc., and
Simon & Schuster, a Division of Gulf & Western Corporation
Simon & Schuster Building
1230 Avenue of the Americas
New York, New York 10020

WINDMILL BOOKS and colophon are trademarks of Windmill Books, Inc.,
registered in the U.S. Patent and Trademark Office.

Manufactured in the United States of America
10 9 8 7 6 5 4 3 2 1

Library of Congress Cataloging in Publication Data

Kraus, Robert, 1925-
    How Spider saved Christmas.

    SUMMARY: Spider thought his Christmas presents
to Fly and Ladybug were unappreciated until the
gifts were used to prevent a diaster.
    [1.   Christmas stories.   2.   Insects—Fiction]
I.   Title.
PZ7.K868Ho   1980   [E]   80-13662

ISBN 0-671-41201-9

It was Christmas Eve and I was feeling sad.

Spiders don't usually celebrate Christmas.
I don't know why. It's just a custom.

Who should I meet in the middle of my sadness
but my two friends, Ladybug and Fly.
"I want you for Christmas dinner," said Ladybug.
"And afterwards we'll go caroling," said Fly.
"You're very kind," I said, "but spiders don't
usually celebrate Christmas."

"Nonsense," said Ladybug. "See you tomorrow
bright and early."
"Bright and early," said Fly as they hurried off.
"Bright and early," I called after them.

I went home and tried to think of what I could
give Fly and Ladybug for Christmas. I knew I
couldn't go empty-handed. I had an old chair
and an old suitcase. I could give Ladybug the
old chair and Fly the old suitcase. But then
what would I sit on or pack my clothes in?

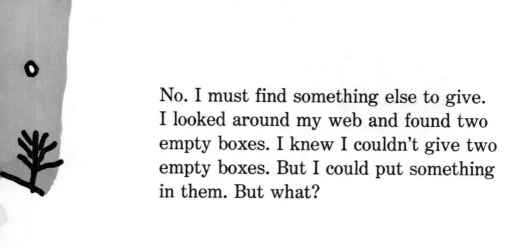

No. I must find something else to give.
I looked around my web and found two
empty boxes. I knew I couldn't give two
empty boxes. But I could put something
in them. But what?

Then in a flash I got an idea.
I filled one box with snow.

I tied it with a ribbon and wrote
To Ladybug—Joyous Yuletide. Your friend Spider.
What a nice present. And what could be more
Christmasy than snow?

But what could I give Fly? More snow? No. It had to be something different. Then I saw some icicles hanging from a tree. That was it! Icicles! Another great idea!

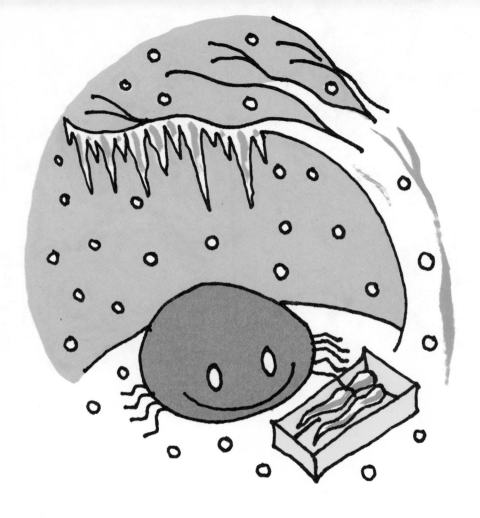

I was very pleased with myself. Christmas
was really fun.

Then with my wrapped presents beside me,
I curled up and fell fast asleep.

Christmas morning shone bright and clear.
Church bells were ringing. Sleigh bells
were tinkling. I felt good as I walked to
Ladybug's house.

I peeked in the window. What a beautiful tree
Ladybug had. Fly was already there having a
cup of tea with Ladybug and stuffing himself
with cookies.
Then I remembered I didn't have to peek.
I was invited!

I knocked at the door.
"Merry Christmas," said Ladybug.
"Merry Christmas," said Fly.
"Merry Christmas," I said.

I put my two presents under the
tree. "It's beautiful," I said.
"Thank you," said Ladybug.
"I helped decorate it," said Fly.

Ladybug handed me a pretty box. "From the bottom of my heart and wear it in good health," she said.

"Thank you," I said. I opened the box. It was
a wool cap.
"It will keep your head warm," said Ladybug.
"I knitted it myself."
"Thank you," I said. "I've always wanted a
warm head."

"From me to you," said Fly.
"Thanks, Fly," I said.

I opened the box. Inside was a snapshot of Fly
in flight.
"It will remind you of me," said Fly.
"Thank you," I said. "Next to a warm head, I've
always wanted to be reminded of you."

Ladybug gave Fly a warm wool scarf.
"I'd sooner had a cap," grumbled Fly.

Fly gave Ladybug a snapshot of himself in flight. It was just like the snapshot he gave me.

"Thank you," said Ladybug. "It will remind me of you."

"That's right," said Fly.

"Now open my presents," I said.
"They seem to be leaking," said Ladybug.
"Leaking is right," said Fly. "It's a flood!"

They opened their presents anyway.

"Water!" said Fly.

"Mine too," said Ladybug. "But be polite."

"Thanks for the water, Spider," said Fly. "It's just what I wanted."

"Yes, thank you," said Ladybug. "Water has so many uses."

"You're very welcome," I said. I was all choked up and I began to cry. My eyes began to smart and burn as if I were in a smoky room. Great Scott! I *was* in a smoky room!

"Ladybug! Ladybug!" I shouted. "Your house
is on fire!"

"It's the stove!" cried Ladybug. "My cupcakes will burn!"

"Let's all run for our lives!" screamed Fly.
"No, wait," I said, calmly grabbing a box of
water. "Do as I do."

"Heave Ho!" I said.
"Heave Ho!" said Fly.
"My poor cupcakes,"
sighed Ladybug.

The fire was put out in no time, but nothing
remained of my presents for Fly and Ladybug
but puddles on the floor and two soggy boxes.
"Gee," I said, "I can't tell you how sorry I am
that your Christmas presents got thrown
on the fire."
"Water he calls Christmas presents,"
muttered Fly.
"Shhh," said Ladybug.
"What I mean is," said Fly, "your Christmas
presents put out the fire and saved the day!"

"Yes, Spider," said Ladybug, kissing me on
the cheek. "You saved the day. You saved
Christmas!"
Well, I guess in a way I did. And I was very
happy I did, because it turned out to be a very
merry Christmas for us all.

THE END